DATE DUE

MAR 24			
OCT 9			
MAR 25			
APR 8			
OCT 21			
OCT 21			
NOV 1			
JAN 20			
FEB 7			
MAR 14			
MAR 24			
OCT 20			
GAYLORD			PRINTED IN U.S.A.

THE
BOLL WEEVIL
Ball

WRITTEN AND ILLUSTRATED BY

Kelly Murphy

HENRY HOLT AND COMPANY

NEW YORK

Henry Holt and Company, LLC
Publishers since 1866
115 West 18th Street
New York, New York 10011
www.henryholt.com

Henry Holt is a registered trademark of Henry Holt and Company, LLC
Copyright © 2002 by Kelly Murphy. All rights reserved.
Distributed in Canada by H. B. Fenn and Company Ltd.

Library of Congress Cataloging-in-Publication Data
Murphy, Kelly.
The boll weevil ball / written and illustrated by Kelly Murphy.
Summary: When a very, very small beetle decides to attend a ball,
he won't let anything stop him—not even the danger of being squished on the dance floor.
[1. Beetles—Fiction. 2. Insects—Fiction. 3. Size—Fiction. 4. Dance—Fiction.] I. Title.
PZ7.M95353 Bo 2002   [E]—dc21   2001005207

ISBN 0-8050-6712-4 / First Edition—2002
The artist used watercolor, gel medium, and acrylic on illustration
board to create the illustrations for this book.
Printed in the United States of America on acid-free paper. ∞
1 3 5 7 9 10 8 6 4 2

For my Mum,
for my Boy

$\mathcal{R}$edd was a small beetle. He was so small he barely fit in the Beetle family picture. Come to think of it, he might have been the smallest beetle ever.

While looking out the window early one morning, Redd noticed a mail bug putting a letter in the mailbox. Maybe it was for him! He raced outside. Then he stacked small stones higher and higher, until he reached the opening. But Redd felt the stones start to tumble, so he grabbed the edge of the mailbox and pulled himself inside.

That was a close call!

Inside the mailbox was an invitation for the Beetles to attend tonight's Boll Weevil Ball. There really wasn't much time to get ready. Redd had to hurry if he wanted to look his absolute best. Using the invitation as a parachute, Redd jumped out of the mailbox and safely floated to the ground.

Redd tried on all his brothers' old
hats and ties, but nothing seemed to fit.
He started to feel discouraged.

A jump in the refreshing
lavender fields and a quick
toothbrushing lifted his
spirits. Redd cleaned
up nicely.

But when Redd wanted to look in the mirror, his big brothers wouldn't budge. He was too small to push them aside, and they were much too busy primping.

Worst of all was when they left Redd behind in their rush to get to the Ball. They had forgotten him, and he didn't know how to fly.

Luckily, a cricket that was one of the
musicians for the Ball hopped by. He might
be Redd's only chance to get there on time. So
Redd gathered up his courage, grabbed hold
of the cricket's leg, and held on for dear life.

After a wild ride, they
finally arrived at the Ball.
Redd discovered that beetles
were definitely not meant to hop.
Feeling a little frazzled, he patiently
waited in line to be greeted by the host. But
the big Boll Weevil didn't notice him, so
Redd just walked inside.

Redd could not have imagined a more beautiful Ball. Lanterns twinkled in the trees, and flowers filled the air with a sweet scent. Music and laughter surrounded the dance floor. Redd scurried to the punch bowl for a cool drink. The cups were bigger than he was, but he was too thirsty to care. As he lifted the heavy cup to his mouth . . .

. . . he, the cup, and all the punch tumbled to the floor.

Suddenly, legs and feet flew at him from all directions.

Redd was in the middle of the dance floor!

He jumped left! He jumped right! He ran forward! BACK! BACK! BACK! Then a bug kicked Redd and his cup off the dance floor. Fortunately, the cup saved him from being squished. Why did he have to be so small? Things can be so hard when you are small. Redd wished he had never come to the Boll Weevil Ball. He climbed a branch to watch everyone else have a good time.

Feeling very sad and lonely, he sat on
the branch.

Then Redd noticed another small bug waving "hello."

 She looked as
delicate as a flower.
She said her name
was Lily, and before Redd could
introduce himself she asked him to
dance. Redd warned her how dangerous
the dance floor was, but Lily just smiled.
She had a surprise.

Lily took Redd's hands, then wings swept the couple off their feet and high into the air. The crowd looked so different from above. But that wasn't the end of her surprise. Suddenly, a bright glow appeared in front of Redd. Lily was a firefly! It was as if they were dancing in their own spotlight.

Redd and Lily danced the Weevil Waltz flawlessly, high above a sea of antennae. The whole crowd watched the two flicker across the night sky. Finally, Redd was as tall as his big brothers.

That night, Redd and Lily flew
and danced till dawn. Redd felt as
though he was the luckiest bug in
the world. And he would never forget
the Boll Weevil Ball.